Scarlett
the Garnet Fairy

by Daisy Meadows

illustrated by Georgie Ripper

Join the **Rainbow Magic Reading Challenge!**

Read the story and collect your fairy points to climb the Reading Rainbow online. Turn to the back of the book for details!

This book is worth 5 points.

The Jewel Fairies

To Josephine Scarlet Whitehouse
– a little jewel, herself

Special thanks to
Sue Mongredien

ORCHARD BOOKS

First published in Great Britain in 2005 by Orchard Books
This edition published in 2016 by The Watts Publishing Group

3 5 7 9 10 8 6 4 2

© 2016 Rainbow Magic Limited.
© 2016 HIT Entertainment Limited.
Illustrations © Georgie Ripper 2005

HIT entertainment

A CIP catalogue record for this book is available from the British Library.

ISBN 978 1 40834 873 4

Printed and bound by CPI Group (UK) Ltd, Croydon, CR0 4YY

The paper and board used in this book are made from wood from responsible sources

Orchard Books
An imprint of Hachette Children's Group
Part of The Watts Publishing Group Limited
Carmelite House, 50 Victoria Embankment, London EC4Y 0DZ

An Hachette UK Company
www.hachette.co.uk
www.hachettechildrens.co.uk

By Frosty magic I cast away
These seven jewels with their fiery rays,
So their magic powers will not be felt
And my icy castle shall not melt.

The fairies may search high and low
To find the gems and take them home.
But I will send my goblin guards
To make the fairies' mission hard.

Contents

A Walk on the Farm

"Wakey, wakey!" Rachel Walker called, bouncing on the end of her friend Kirsty's bed. Kirsty Tate was staying with the Walker family for the October half-term holiday and Rachel didn't want to waste a single second.

Kirsty yawned and stretched. "I just had the most amazing dream," she said sleepily.

"Queen Titania asked us to help the Jewel Fairies find seven stolen gemstones from her magic tiara and…" Her voice trailed away and she opened her eyes wide. "It wasn't a dream, was it?" she said, sitting bolt upright. "We really did meet India the Moonstone Fairy yesterday!"

Rachel nodded, smiling. "We certainly did," she agreed.

Kirsty and Rachel shared a wonderful secret. They were friends with the fairies! They had had all sorts of fantastic adventures with them in the past – and now the fairies were in trouble.

Mean Jack Frost had stolen the seven magical jewels from the Fairy Queen's tiara. He had wanted to keep the jewels for himself, but their magic was so powerful that his ice castle had begun to melt. In a rage, Jack Frost had hurled the jewels away, and now they were lost.

King Oberon and Queen Titania had asked the girls to help return the jewels to Fairyland. Yesterday, Kirsty and Rachel had helped India the Moonstone Fairy find the magic Moonstone. But there were still six jewels left to find.

"I'm glad the Moonstone is safely back in Fairyland," Rachel said. "And I had a lovely dream last night, so we know for sure that India's dream magic is working properly again now."

The Fairy King and Queen had told the girls that the jewels from Queen Titania's tiara controlled some of the most important kinds of fairy magic. Every year, in a special ceremony, the fairies would replenish their magic by dipping their wands in the magical fountain that streamed from the tiara. But Jack Frost had stolen the jewels just before this year's ceremony could take place. And that meant that all the fairies were running low on much of their special fairy magic.

"We've just got to find the other jewels before the fairies' magic is gone," Kirsty said, getting dressed quickly. "Perhaps we'll discover another jewel today!"

Rachel agreed eagerly and together the girls hurried downstairs for breakfast. Unfortunately, it drizzled all morning and there was no sign of any jewels or any fairies.

After lunch, though, the clouds cleared away to reveal a blue sky and sunshine.

"Who wants to come with me to Buttercup Farm?" Mrs Walker asked, clearing away the lunch things.

"We need some vegetables and eggs for tea – and you two look like you need some fresh air."

"We do!" Rachel agreed, grinning at Kirsty. She held up crossed fingers while her mum wasn't looking. "We might come across a jewel," she added in a whisper.

A few minutes later, the girls and Mrs Walker set off down the lane towards the farm. Buttons, the Walkers' dog, trotted happily alongside them, sniffing at interesting smells in the hedgerow.

"He loves coming to the farm," Rachel told Kirsty, patting Buttons. "He's known the Johnsons' sheepdog, Cloud, since they were both pups, and the two of them go crazy whenever they see each other. Don't you, boy?"

"Woof!" barked Buttons, as if he was agreeing with her.

As the girls strolled along, something caught Kirsty's eye. "Look at those," she said, pointing to some red and white toadstools under a tree. "They're exactly like the Fairyland toadstool houses, aren't they?" Rachel nodded. "Oh, I do hope we meet another fairy today, Kirsty!" she said.

Kirsty crunched happily through the fallen leaves. "You know what Queen Titania always says," she whispered, as Mrs Walker bent down and let Buttons off his lead. "Don't go looking for magic…"

"It will find you!" Rachel finished.

Kirsty linked her arm through Rachel's. "It is hard not to look, though," she confessed. "I keep wondering where we're going to meet our next fairy – and who it's going to be!"

"Here we are," Mrs Walker said, as they turned off the lane into a long driveway. An old stone farmhouse stood at the end of the drive, with a pretty thatched roof and wood smoke curling from the chimney.

A smiling woman opened the front door. "Hello," she called warmly. "Come in, all of you. Oh, Buttons, too, Cloud will be pleased."

"This is my friend Kirsty. She's staying with us," Rachel said. "And Kirsty, this is Mrs Johnson."

"Hello," Kirsty said, returning Mrs Johnson's smile.

"Nice to meet you, Kirsty," Mrs Johnson said, leading the way into the sunny farmhouse kitchen. "I've just picked the last plums from my plum tree. Would anyone like one?"

"Yes, please," the girls chorused.

A volley of barking greeted them as they went in, and Cloud, a black and white sheepdog, danced around their legs. Buttons romped joyfully after him, barking just as noisily.

"Shall we take the dogs out for a walk?" Rachel offered quickly, as Buttons' tail almost knocked over a basket of eggs.

"Good idea," Mrs Johnson replied, giving the girls a handful of plums each. "Oh," she added, as they were about to head out of the door, "I should warn you that Mr Johnson is in rather a bad mood. His new green tractor has disappeared and he thinks one of the farm lads has taken it for a ride." She winked at the girls. "So if you see him and he's a bit grumpy, just ignore him, won't you?"

The girls nodded and followed Buttons and Cloud out of the door and into the meadows. Suddenly, Cloud trotted back over to the girls looking very pleased with himself. He dropped something at their feet.

"What's this?" Kirsty asked, bending to pick it up. "Oh, look, Rachel," she said. "It's a tiny toy tractor." She giggled. "Do you think we should give it to Mr Johnson to make up for the one he's lost?"

Rachel grinned. "I don't think he'd appreciate it," she replied. "We'd better leave it here, in case somebody comes back for it."

Kirsty put the tractor down on a flat bit of grass where it was easy to spot. As she straightened up, she noticed some odd-looking, shiny stones. "Are those rocks over there?" she asked in a puzzled voice.

Rachel turned and looked where her friend was pointing. She saw several large brown objects under a chestnut tree on one side of the meadow. "That's strange," she said, frowning. "I've never noticed them before. Let's go and have a closer look."

Kirsty and Rachel ran across to the tree.

The brown objects Kirsty had spotted
were roughly the size and shape of
footballs, and they were
a glossy, chocolate
brown colour.
"Well, they're
not rocks,"
Kirsty said,
stroking one
of them. It felt cool
and smooth under her palm.
"They look more like…giant
chestnuts!"

Rachel patted one curiously.
"They do look like chestnuts," she
agreed. "But whoever heard of a
chestnut this size?"

Before Kirsty could reply, Buttons
bounded over, yapping excitedly.

Then he ran back to a patch of grass a few metres away, sniffed it eagerly and barked again.

Rachel went to see what he'd found. "Kirsty, quick!" she called, her eyes wide. "Come and look at these sheep!"

"Sheep?" echoed Kirsty, incredulously, running over to join Rachel. She couldn't see any sheep, yet as she got nearer to her friend she heard a tiny, but distinct, "Ba-a-a-a-a!"

Rachel pointed down at the grass and Kirsty's gaze followed her finger.

"Tiny sheep!" Kirsty gasped in surprise. "Oh, my goodness! Are they real?"

Down at their feet was a flock of the tiniest sheep Kirsty and Rachel had ever seen. Sheep, the size of mice! Chestnuts, the size of footballs! Whatever was going on?

Rachel's eyes were bright. "There is definitely magic in the air today," she breathed.

"There must be another magic jewel somewhere nearby," Kirsty added, feeling a thrill of excitement.

Hurriedly, the girls put the dogs on their leads and tied them to the fence, so that the tiny sheep would be safe.

Then Rachel clutched Kirsty's arm. "Kirsty!" she squeaked. "Look!"

Both girls stared. Floating down from the chestnut tree in front of them was a large golden leaf — and there, sitting on top of it as if she was riding a magic carpet, was a tiny beaming fairy.

Seeing Red

"Wheeeeee!" squealed the fairy breathlessly. "Hello, girls!"

Kirsty and Rachel laughed in delight as the golden leaf sailed down to the ground. The fairy promptly jumped off and twirled up into the air, her wings beating so quickly they were a blur of glittering colours.

She had curly dark brown hair, and she wore a scarlet dress decorated with a pretty flower where the hemline rose at the front. She also wore little, glittery red shoes which twinkled in the sunlight.

"It's Scarlett the Garnet Fairy," Rachel declared, recognising her instantly. "Hello, Scarlett."

"Of course!" Kirsty said, clapping her hands as she remembered something King Oberon had told them. "The Garnet controls growing and shrinking magic, doesn't it?" she exclaimed. "That's why the chestnuts are so enormous..."

"And the sheep are so tiny," Rachel added, with a smile.

"Exactly," Scarlett said. She waved her wand hopefully, but only a few red sparkles scattered from it. Kirsty watched as they fizzled and spluttered out in the grass. "And unfortunately, without it, I don't have enough magic to turn things back to their proper sizes,"

Scarlett explained sadly.
"We must find the
Garnet before
it changes
anything else."

She flew over to
perch on Kirsty's
shoulder. "India
told me that you had
a run-in with Jack Frost's
goblins yesterday," she said, shivering at
the thought. "Let's try and find the
Garnet before any goblins get here."

"We'll start right away," Rachel said
immediately, and Kirsty nodded.

"Great," Scarlett replied, with a smile.
"I'll try the vegetable patch over there."

"And we'll search this field," Kirsty
said. "Come on, Rachel."

The girls set off across the meadow, scanning the grass for any sign of the Garnet. They were just passing a haystack, when something very strange happened.

"My legs are tingling!" Kirsty gasped.

"We're shrinking!" Rachel cried, as she saw the ground rushing towards her.

The girls had often been fairy-sized before – but then they'd always had pretty wings to fly with too! But not this time – suddenly the haystack seemed like a mountain in front of them, and the grass was waist-high.

"The Garnet must be very close, if the magic is working on us now," Kirsty pointed out.

"Scarlett! Hey, Scarlett!" Rachel shouted, trying to attract the attention of the Garnet Fairy. But her voice had shrunk, too – and Scarlett didn't hear her tiny call.

"Rachel, look at the top of the haystack," Kirsty cried, pointing upwards. "It's glowing red!"

Rachel looked up at once, and sure enough, something at the top of the haystack did seem to be shining a deep red colour. "It must be the Garnet!" she declared. "Let's climb up and get it for Scarlett."

"Good idea," Kirsty agreed.

The two girls began to climb the haystack. It was very hard work because the hay was sharp and slippery and it was difficult to get a firm grip on the smooth stalks, but little by little the girls drew closer to the magic Garnet.

Just as Kirsty was about to reach the top, the stalk she was holding onto suddenly swayed and bent. Kirsty lunged for something else to grab, and clutched at another stalk, but it promptly snapped in two! "Help!" cried Kirsty, desperately trying to hang on. "I'm falling!"

A Scary Surprise

"Here!" Rachel yelled, leaning down to reach Kirsty. "Grab my hand!"

Kirsty clung onto her friend's outstretched fingers, her heart pounding as her feet scrabbled for a safe foothold. "Thanks," she said shakily, as her feet found a strong straw and Rachel helped pull her upwards.

The girls clambered gingerly up the last few steps – and then Rachel gave a triumphant cry. "We've found it!" she cheered, for there in front of them lay the glittering red Garnet. The sun shone through it, casting a rich, rosy light across the hay.

"Wow!" breathed Kirsty. It seemed
even more impressive
now the girls were
fairy-sized. The
jewel was no
bigger than a
hen's egg, but
right now that
was almost as
tall as Rachel
and Kirsty!

"Scarlett!" both
girls shouted. They
waved their arms around
at the top of the haystack, hoping the
fairy would see or hear them.

But Scarlett was still searching hard in
the vegetable patch, completely
unaware that her jewel had been found.

Then Kirsty had a good idea. "What if we turn the Garnet round so that its red light shines across to Scarlett?" she suggested. "That's sure to get her attention."

"Brilliant," Rachel agreed. "I bet it's heavy, though. I think we'll have to lift it together."

Kirsty took hold of one side of the jewel and Rachel held the other. Then, Kirsty counted, "One…two…three!" and together the girls heaved the gemstone around, so that its rosy light was shining directly at Scarlett.

The little fairy turned at once, and when she saw the girls with the Garnet her face lit up. "Yippee!" she cried, leaping into the air and twirling for joy. "Well done!" Kirsty and Rachel both took a hand off the Garnet to wave at her. As they did so, the magic stone slipped slightly and its sparkling red light danced further along the vegetable patch, flickering over a scarecrow that stood nearby.

And then, to the girls' great surprise, the scarecrow moved!

Rachel and Kirsty stared in amazement as the scarecrow jumped down from its wooden stand and started lumbering its way towards the haystack.

"What's happening?" Rachel asked. "Is it more fairy magic, do you think?"

"I don't know," Kirsty replied
doubtfully. "I didn't think the Garnet
could do that." She watched the
scarecrow walking jerkily towards
them, and suddenly felt nervous.
"It's coming over here. What do
you think it wants?"

Rachel narrowed
her eyes and
stared hard at
the scarecrow.
"Hang on a
minute," she said.
"Look at its green,
pointy nose. That's
not a scarecrow — it's a goblin!"

"Oh, no!" Kirsty cried, clutching
Rachel in fright. "Look how
enormous it is!"

"It's as big as a man," Rachel said anxiously, biting her lip. All of a sudden, she felt smaller than ever. How would she and Kirsty protect the Garnet when they were so tiny and the goblin was so huge? "Oh, do be quick, Scarlett! Come and get this Garnet!" she yelled frantically.

Scarlett was flying over as fast as she could, a determined look on her face. "I'm coming," she cried. "Hang on, girls!"

Kirsty gulped, still holding onto Rachel. "Look!" she said, pointing at the scarecrow.

For it had stopped walking and was now pulling off its long coat. And underneath the coat there wasn't just one goblin, there were two – one standing on the other's shoulders. The top goblin jumped down, and as Rachel and Kirsty watched in horror, both goblins started running as fast as they could towards the Garnet – and the girls.

Kidnapped!

"Let's get out of here," Kirsty cried fearfully. As quickly as they could, she and Rachel began to clamber back down the haystack, carrying the Garnet between them. The jewel felt strangely warm as they held it.

"My fingers are tingling," Rachel called out. "Do you think that means—?"

But Rachel's words were cut off, because the Garnet's magic was working again – and this time both girls were growing. They clung tightly to the jewel as their legs lengthened, and their heads shot up towards the sky. Suddenly, the haystack, which had seemed such a mountain to climb, was nothing more than a regular haystack – and it couldn't hold the weight of the two girls. "I'm sinking," Rachel panted, as her feet sunk into the hay. "We're too heavy for the haystack now."

Scarlett arrived at that moment,
her face anxious. "I'll try
and magic you out of
there!" she cried,
waving her wand
quickly. But only one
glittering red sparkle
fell out and fizzled
uselessly on the grass.
"Uh-oh, here come
the goblins!" she
wailed, fluttering
protectively in front
of Kirsty and Rachel.

"Oh dear, oh dear," chortled the taller
goblin who had been at the bottom of
the scarecrow. He watched, sniggering,
as the girls floundered around in the
waist-deep hay.

The other, shorter goblin was close behind. "I think we'll have that Garnet, thank you," he declared, reaching out to snatch it from Rachel's hand.

"Oh, no, you don't!" Rachel cried, throwing the precious stone into the air before the goblin could grab it.

"Catch, Scarlett!"

Scarlett nimbly caught the Garnet just in time, but in the human world it was too big and heavy for her to fly with. She sunk rapidly downwards under the weight of the jewel, desperately flapping her wings as hard as she could.

Kirsty could see that Scarlett was trying to angle her wand so that it would touch the stone, and she realised that the little fairy was hoping to recharge her wand with growing and shrinking magic. But before she could do so, poor Scarlett lost her grip on the wand and it tumbled down into the hay. Luckily, Kirsty pounced on the wand before either of the goblins could reach it, but then something terrible happened. The shorter goblin whipped off the scarecrow hat he still had on his head and held it out beneath the falling fairy.

"Help!" Scarlett cried, as she plunged helplessly into the dark hat.

"Gotcha!" cheered the goblin. "A Garnet and a fairy — that's a bonus!"

"Hey!" called Rachel, kicking out at the hay in an attempt to get free of it. "Bring Scarlett back, right now!"

"No chance!" both goblins laughed nastily — and away they ran.

As the two girls scrambled out of the haystack, the goblins pelted across the field with Scarlett and the Garnet still trapped inside the scarecrow hat. Kirsty and Rachel could hear them singing jubilantly:

"Twinkle, twinkle, Garnet stone,
You are never going home.
Jack Frost wants you hidden away.
Out of Fairyland you shall stay.
Sparkle, sparkle, on and on
The fairies' magic will soon be gone!"

"Come back!" shouted Kirsty angrily.
"Rachel, we've got to get that
scarecrow hat before it's too late!"

Dogs to the Rescue

As Rachel and Kirsty scrambled out
of the hay, they looked wildly
around for anything that would help
them rescue Scarlett. Then Kirsty's
gaze fell upon Cloud and Buttons,
and she remembered that in the past
the goblins had been scared of dogs.
"Wait," she called, thinking fast.

"Maybe Buttons and Cloud can help us!"

The dogs already seemed to have had the same idea. They were both straining at their leads and barking at the goblins.

"Come on, boy," Rachel said, letting Buttons off his lead. "Let's go goblin catching!"

"And you, Cloud," Kirsty said, releasing him too. "Go, dogs, go!" Cloud and Buttons did not need telling twice. With a rousing chorus of barks, they both hurtled eagerly towards the goblins.

The goblin who was carrying the
scarecrow hat looked over his shoulder
and screeched with fear when
he saw the dogs. "Quick!"
he yelled to his friend.
"Get back up the
scarecrow stand!"

Both goblins
scrambled back up
the wooden stand
that had supported
them in their
scarecrow disguise,
and clung tightly
to its beams.

"Woof! Woof! Woof!"
Buttons and Cloud barked
happily, jumping up at the stand
and trying to lick the goblins' toes.

"Eek!" yelped the tall goblin, drawing his feet up. "Shoo, you horrible mutts!"

Kirsty and Rachel ran over. "This is all your fault," they heard the tall goblin hiss at his friend. "It was your idea to climb up here!"

"Well, if you'd run a bit quicker, we could have been out of here by now," the short one moaned back.

"Everything all right?" Kirsty asked sweetly, patting Cloud and Buttons who were still looking hopefully up at the goblins, and wanting to play.

"No!" snapped the tall goblin sulkily.

"Just call the dogs off!" the short goblin begged.

"No chance," Rachel replied cheerfully. "Unless…"

"What? What?" the goblins cried together.

"Unless you set Scarlett free," Kirsty finished.

The short goblin looked thoughtful and scratched his leathery, green head. "All right," he said at last, "the fairy can go – but the Garnet's staying right here, in my hat."

"OK," the girls agreed.

Rachel grabbed both dogs by their collars and held them back. "Now, let Scarlett go," she said.

The goblin cautiously opened the
hat just wide enough for Scarlett
to flutter out.

She zoomed through the
gap and flew to Kirsty's
shoulder. "Thank you,"
she said, as Kirsty
gave her her wand
back. "That
hat smelled awful!"

"Well, you're still not
getting your hands on our jewel," the
goblin said firmly, reaching into the hat
to pat the Garnet protectively, "so you
might as well— Hey!" he suddenly
yelped in surprise. "What's happening?"

Kirsty, Rachel and Scarlett all stared
at the goblin. And then all three of
them began to chuckle.

"It's the Garnet!" Scarlett laughed. "It's making him shrink!"

Sure enough, the short goblin was growing even shorter before their eyes. "Help!  Make it stop!" he squeaked in a tiny voice.

His friend was guffawing loudly – but not for long. Now that there was one big goblin and one tiny goblin on the wooden stand, the whole thing was starting to overbalance.

"Whoa!" the big goblin cried as he felt himself falling. "Help!"

Goblins on the Run

Splat!

The girls backed out of the way just as the large goblin landed heavily on the ground. "Oof!" he panted. "Stupid Garnet!"

"Woof!" barked the dogs, running over and licking the goblin playfully. "Woof! Woof!"

Rachel and Kirsty couldn't help smiling as the goblin rolled around, helpless with laughter. "It tickles!" he roared. "Ooh, it tickles!"

Then Kirsty remembered the Garnet. She rushed over to the scarecrow pole where the tiny goblin was still hanging on – and plucked the hat easily from his grasp.

"Hurrah!" cheered Scarlett as she saw the magic Garnet gleaming in Kirsty's hand. "Well done, Kirsty!"

"We did it!" Rachel beamed. "That's another jewel found."

The girls and Scarlett headed back towards the farmhouse, calling the dogs to follow them once they were a safe distance from the goblins.

Scarlett carefully touched her wand to the magic Garnet and waved it in the air. A stream of glittering, red fairy dust flooded out across the fields and a smile lit Scarlett's face. "That's more like it," she said thankfully.

Baa! Baa! The sheep were suddenly back to their normal size. Cloud and Buttons stared at them in confusion, wondering where they had come from.

Cloud sniffed at a stray red sparkle and jumped as it fizzed into thin air under his nose.

Kirsty turned to look at the chestnut tree. The giant chestnuts had disappeared – they had shrunk to their normal size again – and what was this, standing in the middle of the field?

"Mr Johnson's tractor!" Rachel laughed. "The Garnet must have shrunk that, too – remember we thought it was a toy?"

Kirsty grinned as the last few, bright twinkles of fairy magic disappeared from the tractor's wheels. "Mr Johnson will be in a good mood again, now," she said happily.

"And so will King Oberon and Queen Titania when I magic this Garnet back to Fairyland," Scarlett added.

The tiny goblin had been turned back to his usual size too. The girls and Scarlett watched as he jumped down from the wooden stand and stomped away with his goblin friend. Although the girls couldn't hear what they were saying, it was clear that they were arguing again.

Scarlett chuckled. "And that's the last we'll see of them," she said, sounding satisfied. She touched her wand to the Garnet once more and it vanished in a fountain of glittering red fairy dust.

"And the Garnet's safely back in Fairyland," Rachel commented with a sigh of relief, as the air where the Garnet had been shimmered for a second and then returned to normal.

"And I should be going back too," Scarlett added, hugging the girls goodbye. "Thank you for all your help, Kirsty and Rachel. And good luck finding the other magic jewels!"

The girls waved as the tiny fairy

zoomed away to Fairyland.

"Phew," Rachel said, as they neared the farmhouse. "That was close. I thought the goblins were going to get away with the Garnet *and* Scarlett then."

Kirsty ruffled Cloud's shaggy coat affectionately. "Well, thanks to these two dogs, both Scarlett and the Garnet are safe and sound," she declared with a smile.

Rachel grinned at Kirsty. "Come on," she said, breaking into a run. "I'm starving. I wonder if Mrs Johnson has got any of those plums left."

"I hope so," Kirsty said, running towards the house. "Race you there!"

**Now Rachel and Kirsty
must help...**

Emily the Emerald Fairy

Read on for a sneak peek...

"Wow!" Kirsty Tate gasped, her
eyes wide with amazement. "This is
the biggest toy shop I've ever seen!"

Her best friend, Rachel Walker,
laughed. "I know," she agreed.
"It's brilliant, isn't it?"

Kirsty nodded. Wherever she turned,
there was something wonderful to see.
In one corner of the toy shop was an
enormous display of dolls in every shape
and size, together with a spectacular
array of dolls' houses.
A special, roped-off area was filled with

remote-control cars, buses, lorries and aeroplanes, and nearby stood rows of bikes, trikes and silver scooters.

Shelves were piled high with every single board game Kirsty had ever heard of, stacks of electronic games and a variety of computer consoles. Colourful kites hung from the ceiling, along with multi-coloured balloons and marvellous mobiles. Kirsty had never seen anything like it, and this was only the ground floor!

"Look over there, Kirsty," Rachel said, pointing at the dolls.

Kirsty saw a sign saying, *Meet Fairy Florence and her friends*. She stared at the dolls grouped around the sign. Fairy Florence wore a long pink dress, and looked rather dull and old-fashioned. Kirsty and Rachel glanced at each other and burst out laughing.

"Fairy Florence doesn't look anything like a real fairy!" Rachel whispered, and Kirsty nodded.

Rachel and Kirsty knew what real fairies looked like because they'd met them, many times. The two girls had often visited Fairyland to help their friends when they were in trouble. The cause of the problem was usually cold, spiky Jack Frost, who was always making mischief with the help of his mean goblin servants...

Read Emily the Emerald Fairy
to find out what adventures are in store for Kirsty and Rachel!

Meet the
Friendship Fairies

When Jack Frost steals the Friendship Fairies' magical objects, BFFs everywhere are in trouble! Can Rachel and Kirsty help save the magic of friendship?

www.rainbowmagicbooks.co.uk

Calling all parents, carers and teachers!
The Rainbow Magic fairies are here to help
your child enter the magical world of reading.
Whatever reading stage they are at, there's
a Rainbow Magic book for everyone!
Here is Lydia the Reading Fairy's guide to
supporting your child's journey at all levels.

Starting Out

1 Our Rainbow Magic Beginner Readers are perfect for first-time readers who are just beginning to develop reading skills and confidence. Approved by teachers, they contain a full range of educational levelling, as well as lively full-colour illustrations.

Developing Readers

2 Rainbow Magic Early Readers contain longer stories and wider vocabulary for building stamina and growing confidence. These are adaptations of our most popular Rainbow Magic stories, specially developed for younger readers in conjunction with an Early Years reading consultant, with full-colour illustrations.

Going Solo

3 The Rainbow Magic chapter books - a mixture of series and one-off specials - contain accessible writing to encourage your child to venture into reading independently. These highly collectible and much-loved magical stories inspire a love of reading to last a lifetime.

www.rainbowmagicbooks.co.uk

"Rainbow Magic got my daughter reading chapter books. Great sparkly covers, cute fairies and traditional stories full of magic that she found impossible to put down" - Mother of Edie (6 years)

"Florence LOVES the Rainbow Magic books. She really enjoys reading now" Mother of Florence (6 years)

Read along the Reading Rainbow!

Well done – you have completed the book!

This book was worth 1 star.

See how far you have climbed on the Reading Rainbow.
The more books you read, the more stars you can colour in
and the closer you will be to becoming a Royal Fairy!

Do you want to print your own Reading Rainbow?

1) Go to the Rainbow Magic website

2) Download and print out the poster

3) Colour in a star for every book you finish
and climb the Reading Rainbow

4) For every step up the rainbow,
you can download your very own certificate

There's all this and lots more at
rainbowmagicbooks.co.uk

You'll find activities, stories, a special newsletter
AND you can search for the fairy with your name!